What's a Fraggle?

By Louise Gikow · Pictures by Barbara McClintock

Muppet Press
Holt, Rinehart and Winston
NEW YORK

Published by Holt, Rinehart and Winston,
383 Madison Avenue, New York, New York 10017.

Library of Congress Cataloging in Publication Data
Gikow, Louise.
What's a Fraggle?
Summary: Describes in rhyme the Fraggles and where they live.
[1. Puppets—Fiction. 2. Stories in rhyme] I. McCue,
Lisa, ill. II. Title.
PZ8.3.G376Wh 1984 [E] 83-22779
ISBN 0-03-071086-3
First Edition
Printed in the United States of America
1 3 5 7 9 10 8 6 4 2

ISBN 0-03-071086-3

What's a Fraggle?

JUST a little west of somewhere
And a little north of here,
Just a little left of center,
Not too far, but not too near—

SOME~
WHERE
HERE
CENTER
N
W
E
S

There's a secret, special somewhere
Near a workshop owned by Doc,
Full of pools and stones and caverns
That is known as Fraggle Rock.

Through a hole and down a tunnel
Is where Fraggle Rock is found,
And a thousand thousand Fraggles
Live there safely underground.

"What's a Fraggle?" you might giggle.
"It's a very silly name.
I don't think I've ever seen one.
Are they wild, or are they tame?"

"What's a Fraggle?" you might question
With a wiggle of your nose.
"I know all the animaggles
But I've never heard of those."

Well, the Fraggles all are fuzzy
And their size is in-between
And they come in many colors—
Yellow, pink, red, blue, and green.

And the Fraggles *are* a giggle,
For they love to laugh and play.
And when Fraggles finish breakfast
Games and music fill the day!

Now, of all the furry Fraggles
There are five whom you should know.
They are Gobo, Mokey, Boober,
Red, and Wembley—there they go!

These five Fraggles stick together
When a problem is in sight.
And they're best of buddies, even
In their Fraggle dreams at night.

Gobo is a brave explorer,
Crossing streams and climbing rocks.

While old Boober would much rather
Stay at home and wash his socks.

Mokey Fraggle is a poet
And her verses are sublime!
(Do you know what rhymes with *radish?*
That one stumps her every time.)

CADISH
BADISH
MADDISH
SADDISH
GLADISH

Wembley always says, "I'll do it!"
For he doesn't like to fight.
And he's not good on decisions—
'Cause he might not...but he might!

Red's an athlete of distinction
And she swims and dives with grace.
Though she has been known, from time to time,
To fall flat on her face.

"Is a Fraggle," you might wonder,
"Like an otter or a seal?
Now, I wouldn't want to haggle
But are Fraggles really real?"

Well, you just might meet a Fraggle
In Hong Kong, New York, or Perth,
For one of them, called Uncle Matt,
Has been exploring Earth!

But if ever you're in Doc's place,
Keep an eye out for our crew,
For the Fraggles down in Fraggle Rock
Are just as real as you!